This book
belongs to

_____

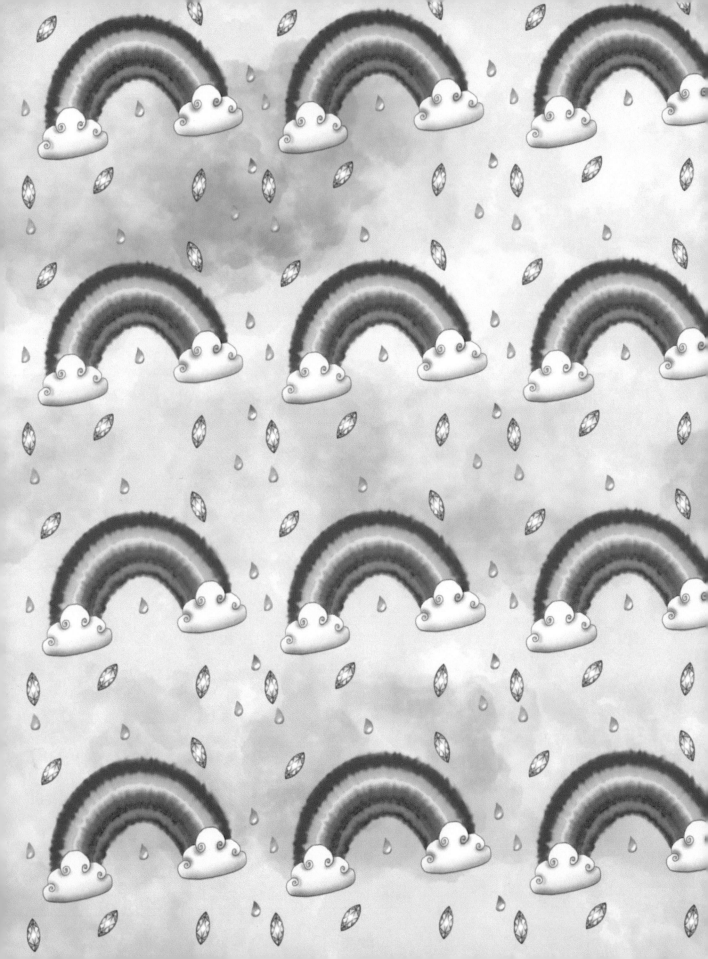

This book is dedicated to
my grandson, Theo

Illustrated by Diana Rozevskis (aka DiArts)

THE RAINBOW

Story by
Christina Baker

Illustrated by
Diana Rozevskis

Theo looked out at the grey cloudy day
and thought he would stay inside and play.

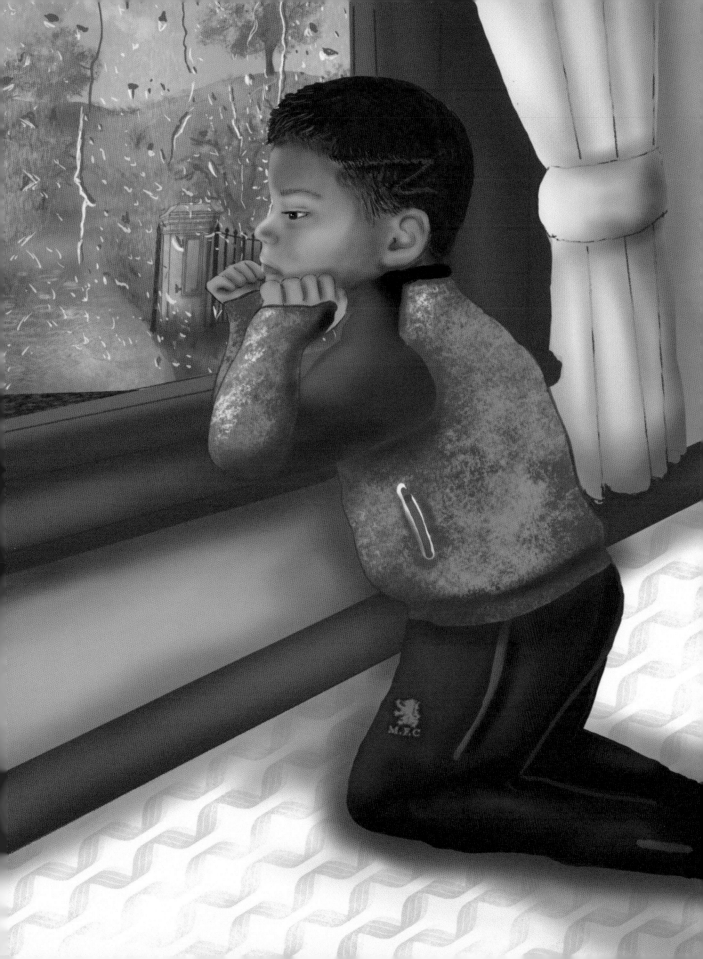

He thought about his books,

his planes,

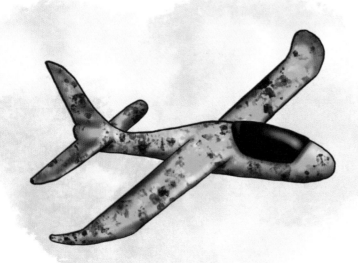

and his cars.

And flying a rocket ship
up to the stars.

Then he spied from the corner of his eye,
the sun began to shine in a deep blue sky.

And as the rain began to fall like tears,
suddenly, he saw a rainbow appear.

He ran to his mum and said,
"Mum, come and see, there's
a rainbow hanging over that
big old tree."

"I'll climb the tree," he said,
"to the top I will go. I'll be so high,
touch the sky and catch
the rainbow."

"I will use the rainbow as a slide
and slip down to the other side."

As he pulled on his boots,
he shouted to Mum,
"Let's go. Hurry up now.
Come on Mum, come!"

"Hmmm!" said Mum,
and took her coat
near the door.
"OK, that sounds like fun,
let's go and explore."

So, Theo put on his jacket

 and Mum, her scarf.

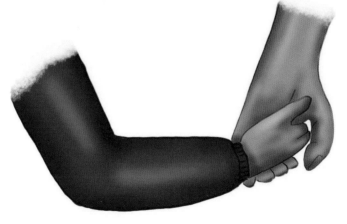

And he held her hand all the way to the park.

There, Theo ran to catch the rainbow, at last.

And as the sky turned bluer
and the sun got strong.
Theo reached the tree
and the rainbow... it was gone!

Theo flopped down on the grass feeling glum,
when a little old lady said,
"Now come, young man, come."

"Don't give up now," she said,
"don't look sad. I know what you want,"
as she reached in her bag.

Out of it she pulled a long piece of string,
and on the end was a glass sparkly thing.

"This is a crystal," the old lady beamed,
and held it up to the light as it gleamed.

"Now then, Young Man, you
can take off that frown,
pick yourself up and
have a good look around."

So, up he got and laughed when he found -
tiny rainbows shimmered on the ground.

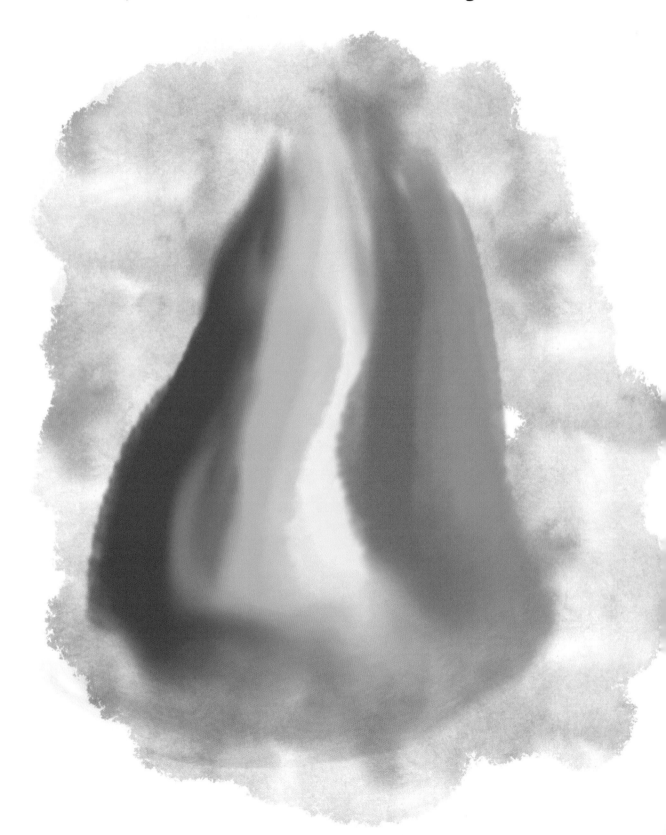

"Mum!" shouted Theo, "look, isn't it grand?"
as the old lady placed it into his hand.

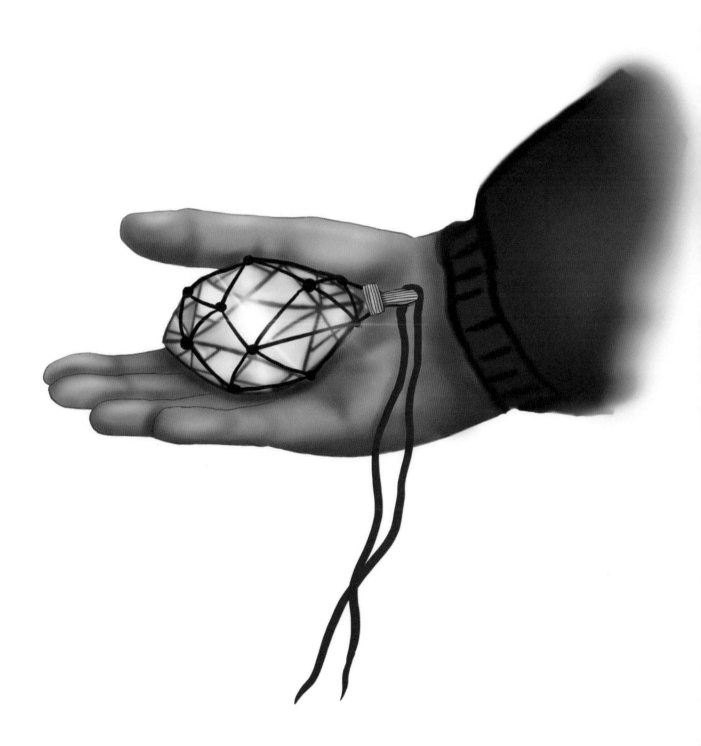

"Well, well!" smiled Mum,
although they're quite small,
I'd say you caught your
rainbow after all."

Printed in Great Britain
by Amazon